QUICKREADS

THE
MYSTERY
QUILT

JANET LORIMER

SADDLEBACK
EDUCATIONAL PUBLISHING

◼QUICKREADS

SADDLEBACK
EDUCATIONAL PUBLISHING
www.sdlback.com

Copyright ©2010, 2002 by Saddleback Educational Publishing

ISBN-13: 978-1-61651-183-8
ISBN-10: 1-61651-183-4
eBook: 978-1-60291-905-1

Printed in Guangzhou, China
0411/04-80-11

15 14 13 12 11   2 3 4 5 6

■ ■ ■

A doll-size pink dress plopped onto the page of Rachel's book. Rachel gazed up at her mother in bewilderment.

Mrs. Butler smiled widely. "Look! You wore that little dress when you were a baby, just six months old," she said. "Your grandmother made it for you—you know, to wear for special occasions."

Mrs. Butler picked up the tiny dress again and gazed at it fondly. "You looked adorable in it."

Rachel raised one eyebrow. "Just how many 'special occasions' can there be for a six-month-old?" she asked.

Mrs. Butler ignored the sarcasm. "The

thing is, the dress is stained. I can't pass it on to any other baby. But I thought we could find a square of good material in it." Rachel raised her other eyebrow in question. "It's for the quilt," Mrs. Butler explained. "Remember? This Saturday is your birthday. Surely you remember, Rachel—the tradition!"

Rachel sighed when she heard the excitement in her mother's voice. She hadn't forgotten. On Saturday, she would turn 20. By tradition, that was the day she would add a square to the family's special birthday quilt.

Rachel closed her book. "Mom—" she began, but her mother interrupted.

"I do not want to hear the word 'no,'" Mrs. Butler said firmly. "You *know* how much the quilt tradition means to this family. Now please think about the square you want to add."

She handed Rachel a large box. "These are some of your other things I've saved over the years. If you'd rather use one of them—that's fine. But you have to pick out something."

Mrs. Butler marched out of the room. Rachel slid down in her chair with a groan. "Why now?" she thought.

The book she'd been holding fell off her lap. Rachel picked it up, gazing in misery at the title. The book was about America a century ago. It was so boring it almost put her to sleep. She had been struggling to read it because she hoped it would inspire her. She needed a term-paper topic for her least favorite class.

Rachel was a business major at the local community college. She'd worked hard to earn several scholarships. She also held down a job while she went to school. If she could get through this semester, she'd be able to transfer to the state university. But that depended on how well she did in American history—the one subject she hated.

Rachel was a go-getter. She didn't believe in looking backward. "I have to keep moving ahead, thinking of the future," she often told herself. "What does history have to do with that?"

She put the book down and lifted the lid of the box. Inside, wrapped in tissue, she found a pair of yellow corduroy overalls. When she held them up, she saw a faint grass stain on one knee and a small patch on the other.

She grinned, remembering. "I was running from my cousin on the grass when I fell. How old was I?" She struggled to recall. "Three? Four?"

The next garment was a blue plaid blouse she'd worn when she was seven. "It was my favorite," she thought. "I wanted to wear it every day. Mom had to fight me to get it in the wash."

There were a couple of other shirts and dresses, but Rachel didn't bother with them. The plaid blouse was her choice for the quilt square.

Then she remembered that she'd planned to spend Saturday at the library working on that term paper. "And I *still* don't have a subject!" she exclaimed out loud. With a deep sigh, she gazed at the small pile of clothes in her lap, worrying about her schedule.

Mom would expect her to spend Saturday with Grandma. It wouldn't take long to stitch Rachel's cloth square onto the quilt. But Grandma would want them to stay for a visit. She missed seeing family.

"Saturday is shot," Rachel thought unhappily. "That means I can't really get going on the paper until next week."

She leaned back, staring at the ceiling, but not seeing it. "American history!" she muttered. "Revolutionary War. Civil War—" Rachel made a face.

"Also known as the War Between the States," she mused. "That was when my people were all slaves!"

Rachel's ancestors had been kidnapped from their homes in Africa and brought in chains to America. Rachel shuddered. "I will *not* write about the Civil War," she thought angrily. "The subject is just too upsetting. Besides, it's long past. Let's look ahead."

In the 1900s, two world wars had been fought! "A lot of wars," Rachel thought in disgust. Then there was the Great

Depression. Prohibition. The Roaring Twenties and the Wild Sixties. She sighed. None of those eras inspired her.

Rachel picked up the plaid blouse and studied it. She had an idea. What about a topic like "fashions through the ages"? That might work.

It made her think of the squares in the family quilt. Squares dating back to—Rachel frowned. She'd never paid much attention when her mother and grandmother talked about the family history. Maybe it was time to take a closer look at the birthday quilt.

After dinner, Rachel and her mother brought the quilt downstairs. Rachel could smell the strong odor of mothballs as her mother lifted the quilt from layers of tissue paper. She and her mother spread it out on the dining room table.

Rachel gave a low whistle. She recognized some of the newer squares. There was her mother's square, a red and white stripe. Grandma's square was a faded navy blue silk. Aunts and cousins had also contributed, as well as some great-great-...Suddenly Rachel paused. It had never occurred to her before just how *old* the quilt must be!

At the center were the oldest squares. The fabric was so old and thin, Rachel was almost afraid to touch it. But she couldn't resist letting her fingertips lightly caress the cloth.

"She touched this cloth," Rachel said. "Imagine that! The woman who started this quilt, whoever she was!" She looked questioningly at her mother. "Mom? Do you know anything about her?"

Mrs. Butler shrugged. "Only that she was an ancestor named Sarah. I'm sure your grandma can tell you more."

Rachel was surprised to realize that she was looking forward to Saturday. Now she was really curious!

■ ■ ■

"**W**hy twenty?" she asked her mother as they drove to the nursing home on Saturday. "Why do we sew in a new square when we turn twenty? What's so important about that birthday?"

Mrs. Butler sighed. "I don't know," she said. "I never really thought about it. I'm sure my mother told me, but—" She shrugged.

Rachel laughed. "I'm going to remember this conversation the next time you get on my case about not paying attention in history class."

When they got to the nursing home, Grandma Hutcherson was waiting for them. She gave Rachel a big hug and thrust a gift-wrapped package into her hand. "This is for my sweet birthday girl," she said with a warm smile.

Rachel tore off the paper. It was a new yellow sweater her grandmother had knitted. Rachel held it up. "Grandma, you always give me what I want most," she said with a laugh. "No birthday would be complete without a beautiful new sweater."

"It's become a tradition, hasn't it?" Mrs. Butler added.

A tradition! Rachel pulled up a chair close

to her grandmother's rocker. "What can you tell me about the birthday quilt?" she asked. "Mom says that it's really old, and that one of our ancestors sewed it, but—" She lifted her shoulders in a shrug. "Where did it come from? Why is it so important? What—"

Mrs. Hutcherson laughed and held up her hands as if to protect herself. "Slow down, child. I'm glad to see you're interested in that quilt. As for who made it, that was Sarah, my great-, great-, great—" Her eyes crinkled up at the corners as her smile widened. "My many-times-great-grandmother."

"What do you know about her?" Rachel asked.

Mrs. Hutcherson thought for a moment. "Sarah was born into slavery," the old woman said softly.

Rachel felt herself tense. She was sure she wasn't going to like this story very much. But as her grandmother talked, Rachel found herself drawn into Sarah's story.

Grandma Hutcherson knew only what she'd been told by her own grandmother.

Sarah had been born about 1830 on a cotton plantation in the South.

Life had been horrible for Sarah and the other slaves. Slave children were not educated. Many slave owners didn't want their slaves even to figure out just where they were. If they did, they might try to escape. Besides, all the owners agreed that slaves were meant to work, not learn. Education didn't make sense.

When the slave children were old enough, they were forced into labor. They had to work long hours, rain or shine, even when they were sick. They had very little food and usually lived in terrible conditions.

When Sarah was five, her mother died in childbirth. Later, Sarah's father was sold to another planter.

Bitter tears stung Rachel's eyes. She could imagine the pain the little girl must have felt when she lost her mother and then her father. There was already the pain from hunger and the pain from whippings if she didn't do what she was told. So much pain for someone so young!

Sarah was chosen to be a "sewing slave." Her job was to make clothing for the members of the family that owned her. And Sarah also made quilts.

"Sarah was a good seamstress," Grandma Hutcherson said. "Her stitches were so fine and tiny they were almost invisible. That's why she sewed many beautiful quilts for her owner's family."

Grandma Hutcherson saw the glint of tears in Rachel's eyes. She took her granddaughter's hand in hers. "Come on, child. Let's get to work on your quilt square," she said softly.

Rachel wiped away the tears. She showed her grandmother the blue plaid square she'd cut out so carefully. "But my stitches aren't very small," Rachel warned with a shaky laugh. "Please don't expect my sewing to be as fine as Sarah's was!"

Now, as Rachel gazed at the quilt, she felt sick. "Did Sarah make this quilt for the family that owned her?" she demanded.

Grandma's eyes widened. "Oh, no, child! No, this quilt was made for a different reason—a special reason. That's the good part of the story.

"Sarah ached to be free. She knew that if she could get to Canada, she could have a new life. But getting there was another story. Slaves who ran away were hunted down like animals. If they were caught, they were whipped or tortured. Sometimes they were branded on the cheek with the letter R, which stood for *runaway*.

"But Sarah had also heard stories about slaves who made it to Canada on the Underground Railroad."

"Of course, you know it wasn't really a railroad," Mrs. Butler explained to Rachel. "And it wasn't underground."

Rachel grinned at her mother. "History may not be my best subject, but I do know that, Mom! I know that the Underground Railroad was a network of safe-houses. Those were secure places where runaways could rest and get dry clothing and food."

Mrs. Butler nodded. "The safe-houses were called 'stations,'" she said. "The people who helped the slaves escape were 'conductors.' And the escaping slaves were known as 'packages.' That's how they communicated secretly. They said one thing, but meant another."

"Some folks called the Underground Railroad the Freedom Train," Grandma said. Her needle whipped in and out of the blue plaid fabric. "Rachel, do you know about Harriet Tubman?"

Rachel frowned. "I remember one of my teachers talking about her. She was—" Then Rachel made a face and shrugged. "I guess that's a part of history I overlooked."

Grandma clicked her tongue in disapproval. "Rachel, you need to know about the past before you can figure out where you're going."

"That's what I keep telling her," Mrs. Butler said with a sigh.

Rachel glanced from her mother to her grandmother. "Hey! You guys are ganging up on me!" she laughed. "Okay—tell me about Harriet Tubman."

"Harriet Tubman was a slave who escaped to the North," Grandma said. "But once she was free, she went back into the South to guide more slaves to freedom. Every time she made that trip, she risked her life. Her people called her *Moses*. She was a remarkable woman."

In an hour or so, Rachel's square had been added to the quilt. As she and her mother gently folded the quilt, Rachel said, "But I still don't know what's so important about *this* quilt."

Grandma Hutcherson's dark eyes widened. "Oh, child, I guess I left out the most important part. This quilt was—"

All of a sudden she stopped talking. A sly grin transformed her face. "Why, this quilt has a *secret,* Rachel," she continued. "You said you're writing a paper for a history class? That's what you should write about."

"Well, what *is* the secret?" Rachel asked impatiently.

Her grandmother shook her head. "I think you better do some digging on your own, child. You can find out for yourself what that secret was all about."

"Can't you just tell me about it now?" Rachel begged. "My paper is due in less than a week, Grandma. I need all the help I can get."

"Honey, it's late, and your grandma's tired," Mrs. Butler said gently. "We can come back next Saturday, and—"

Rachel groaned. "Mom, I have to turn my term paper in on *Friday*. Saturday will be too late!"

■ ■ ■

On Monday morning, Rachel went straight to the college library. She cornered a reference librarian and explained her problem.

"There are some fascinating books on quilting," the librarian said. "You can also do some research on the Internet. But why don't we start with what you already know about your ancestor."

Grandma had mentioned that Sarah was born on the Hardee plantation. By doing a little digging, Rachel discovered that the plantation house had been turned into a museum and education center. That night, when she told her mother, Mrs. Butler got excited.

"Why don't we drive down there tomorrow?" Rachel asked. Mrs. Butler quickly agreed.

To Rachel's surprise, the Hardee plantation house was not a fancy two-storied white mansion. It was a single-story wooden house—now painted yellow with white trim.

"I guess I was expecting a mansion from *Gone With the Wind*," Rachel said.

Their tour guide, John Whitman, laughed. "No, this was never a huge plantation," he said. "Most Southern plantations weren't as large and fancy as the one in *Gone With the Wind*. And not all white Southerners owned slaves."

As they walked through the rooms of the

house, John talked a little about himself. He was a student at state university, majoring in black studies.

"I volunteer here as often as I can," he said. "I like to take school groups around the plantation and tell them the history. I love seeing the 'aha' looks on all the kids' faces when they learn something new."

Rachel smiled. "You may see a lot of 'aha' looks on *my* face. History has never seemed very interesting to me until just recently." Then she told him about the family quilt.

John was fascinated. "Sounds like your family treasure might have started as an encoded quilt," he said.

Rachel's eyes widened. "What do you mean—that it contained a code?"

"Many people believe," John said, "that the abolitionists—"

"The what?" Rachel cut in.

"The people who worked to abolish slavery," John explained. "They were free blacks and whites. Abolitionists were the people who helped slaves escape. It's said that they used quilts as maps."

"Oh, yes, I've heard that story," Mrs. Butler said.

"The story of the map-quilts was handed down from one generation to another," John said. "Some people say it doesn't count, because it's only oral history. But that's how many cultures around the world have passed on information and tradition—through oral history.

"The quilt code was a secret language. It had to be that way. The abolitionists didn't dare talk about their activities out loud. What they were doing was against the law. If they were caught, they, too, would have been punished."

"So *nothing* was written down?" Rachel asked.

John shrugged. "So it would seem. That's why there's some controversy. But most people believe the oral tradition is as sound as any written document."

In one of the bedrooms, Rachel saw a

quilt folded neatly across the foot of the bed. She wondered if Sarah might have sewn it for one of her white owner's children. "This quilt was nothing but a quilt," John said, seeing the look on her face. "Wait until we go outside."

Next, he took them on a tour of the outbuildings. These included small cabins where slave families had lived. Most of the cabins had held two families, so the people had no privacy. Worse, the crudely built cabins were cold in the winter and hot in the summer.

Rachel gazed in despair at the dirt floor and leaky ceiling. "No human being should ever have to live in such terrible conditions," she thought.

Outside one of the slave cabins, a quilt hung over a railing. "This isn't a real slave quilt," John said. "Any original slave quilts that survived are too fragile to be displayed like this. But it's a good copy. Notice the design?"

Rachel nodded and shrugged. "Do you

know what it means?"

John laughed. "If you were the overseer or a slave hunter, you wouldn't have thought anything about it. Not even if you saw this quilt hanging out to air. But to the slaves it was a signal. It meant that someone was coming to help them escape."

"On the Underground Railroad!" Rachel exclaimed. "I get it. Wow! What a story of intrigue!"

John nodded. "When I think about the risks, the dangers, I wonder if I could have been so brave. Did you know that one slave actually crated and shipped himself to Philadelphia?"

"That was pretty darn clever—or desperate," Rachel said, shuddering.

"You said your ancestor fled north from here," John said. "There may be records of her escape."

Rachel sighed. "I'd love to read those records, John—but I'm running out of time." Then she told him about the paper that was due on Friday.

John grinned. "Tell you what," he said. "Let me help. History is my favorite subject. I can comb through the old plantation records while you check out the Underground Railroad."

Rachel accepted his offer with a big smile of gratitude.

"Where did the Underground Railroad start, John?" Mrs. Butler asked.

"There wasn't just one starting point," John told her. "About 1831, people called 'travelers' started coming South to teach the slaves the routes to follow. The slaves then passed that information on to other slaves by using codes in songs. Do you know the folk song, 'Follow the Drinking Gourd'?"

Rachel nodded. "I've heard it sung. What about it?"

"The drinking gourd was a code phrase for the Big Dipper and the North Star," John explained. "The position of the stars gave escaping slaves a direction to follow. 'Follow the Drinking Gourd' was the route for an escape from Alabama to Mississippi."

He handed Rachel a sheet of paper. "This is a map of the Underground Railroad routes. And here's a list of homes that are now historic sites."

"Look, Rachel," her mother said, pointing to an address on the list. "The Warren house is on our way home. Why don't we go there next?"

Rachel nodded. John looked at the expression on her face, and his smile widened. "I do believe I see an 'aha' look right now!" he laughed.

Rachel grinned. "History used to seem so boring," she told him. "I always hated it. But now—"

"It's become personal," John said with a nod. "The more we learn, the more our ancestors come to life and become more than names or photos. Then we can see them as people with feelings and interesting lives of their own."

"I still have a lot more to learn about Sarah," Rachel said, "but now it's like an exciting mystery story. I keep finding new clues! I just hope they unravel the mystery of her quilt."

■ ■ ■

An hour later, Rachel and her mother drove up to the Warren House.

Although a marker telling about the Underground Railroad stood outside, the house itself was privately owned. Rachel felt a little nervous when she knocked on the front door. But the present owner—Mary O'Brien—was delighted to show Rachel and her mother the secret room under the barn. This was where the slaves had hidden before going on to the next safe-house.

"The couple who owned the house before the Civil War—the Warrens—were Quakers," Mary said. "They were very kind people who helped many runaway slaves. And of course that put them in plenty of personal danger."

"But they weren't caught, were they?" Rachel asked.

Mary nodded. "Just before the Civil War broke out, Mr. Warren was caught smuggling a slave to the next safe-house. He was arrested and fined by the local judge. But that didn't stop him. Mr. Warren and his wife went right on helping slaves escape. They were lucky to only pay a fine! They could have been imprisoned or killed."

Rachel gazed about the small dark room. She tried to imagine how it would feel to be hiding here. As they drove to the Warren house, she and her mother had talked about the months it took to get from the Southern states to Canada. Most escaping slaves had been forced to walk hundreds of miles.

Slaves were sometimes encouraged to escape during winter. It was easier to cross a frozen river than to swim it in the summer. Rachel wondered how many escaping slaves had died along the way—from accidents, snakebite, or even the cold? Not to mention the ones who got caught! Rachel shivered.

Mary saw Rachel's reaction. "It was a sad and shameful time in America," Mary said. "Slavery was here before the American Revolution. Even some of our founding fathers—men like George Washington and Thomas Jefferson— owned slaves." She shook her head.

"Thank goodness slavery was finally abolished in America," Mrs. Butler exclaimed. "I know that slavery still exists today in some other countries. I think that's what your grandma meant, Rachel—about knowing the past before you can look to the future."

Rachel nodded. "It sure makes me feel differently about history," she said. "But right now, my problem is the secret in Sarah's quilt."

"You've learned a lot in just a couple of days," her mother said. "Maybe you can persuade Grandma to tell you the rest of the story now."

■ ■ ■

Grandma Hutcherson was waiting for Rachel.

"How did you know I was coming?" Rachel exclaimed. "Did Mom phone you when I left the house?"

Grandma Hutcherson laughed and shook her head. "I just had a feeling that you might come today. Come here, child. I have a lot to show you."

When Rachel sat down, Grandma Hutcherson reached in her pocket and handed Rachel an old locket. "Do you remember this?" the old woman asked.

"I've seen you wear it lots of times," Rachel said. "I remember seeing it when I was little. You'd open it and show me pictures inside. I thought it was so neat the way it opened. Like a little door."

Grandma opened the locket. "This is Sarah," she said, pointing to the old sepia-colored photograph. "And that's her husband," Grandma added. "He would be your great-, great-, many-times-great-grandfather."

Rachel drew her breath in sharply. She reached out to touch the glass over the photo. The people in the photograph had meant nothing until now. But today—maybe for the first time in her life—Rachel felt a close link with her many-times-great-grandparents. It was as if she could look back across the ages and see them smiling at her.

"Now I'll tell you the rest of the story," Grandma said softly.

She explained that Sarah sewed quilts for her owner and quilts for her own people. The quilts for her people had messages encoded in the designs. The "flying geese" design represented the wings of freedom. It was also a compass.

The log cabin design usually had a red or yellow square in the center of each cloth block. "Red meant the hearth," Grandma said. "Yellow was a lighted window. But the coded quilts had a black square in the center of each block of cloth. That stood for a safe-house."

Rachel gasped. What Sarah had been sewing were freedom quilts!

When she was 19 years old, Sarah had escaped from the Hardee plantation. It took her months to reach Canada—months of sheer terror and exhaustion, every hour of every day fearing injury or capture or death.

"She set foot on Canadian soil on her twentieth birthday," Grandma said.

Rachel felt her heart pounding.

Grandma chuckled. "On Saturday, I asked your mother to leave the birthday quilt with me," she said. "I want you to look at it again. And this time, you need to take a closer look."

Together, they carefully unfolded the quilt. Now when Rachel looked at the earliest squares and their designs, she saw more than a quilt. Sarah had made a stitched record of her journey from slavery to freedom.

"Sarah sewed many quilts for many people for many reasons," Grandma said. "I'm told that she started *this* quilt on the day she reached freedom. It was then that Sarah vowed that her children and their children and their children's children would each add a square."

"I understand, Grandma," Rachel whispered, her eyes bright with pride. "It's not just to celebrate our twentieth birthdays, it's to celebrate our freedom."

After-Reading Wrap-Up

1. Why were runaway slaves often encouraged to travel in winter rather than summer?

2. After reading *The Mystery Quilt,* would you agree with Rachel that history can be interesting? Explain your answer.

3. Rachel is reluctant to hear about slavery. She finds the subject too painful. What do you think of her attitude?

4. Grandma tells Rachel, "You need to know about the past before you can figure out where you're going." Do you agree or disagree? Give reasons for your answer.

5. Why wouldn't Grandma tell Rachel the full story of the quilt when Rachel first asked her?

6. When did Sarah begin the quilt that became Rachel's family treasure?